At the House of the Safe Witch

Sheila K. McCullagh

Illustrated by Pat Cook

Nelson

After breakfast, Tim cut himself a thick sandwich of bread and cheese. He put it in a paper bag, and pushed it into the pocket of his jacket.

Aunt May gave him an apple. He knew that she was always glad when he went out for the day. He didn't mind that. He knew that she was thinking of the lodgers. She was worried about Miss Miff.

Aunt May always said, "The less Miss Miff sees of you, Tim, the better. She just doesn't like boys. She pays well, and we need the money. I don't want her to leave."

Tim didn't like Miss Miff any more than Miss Miff liked him. He was always glad to get out of the house, or up to his own room out of her way, and today he wanted to get away as soon as he could. He wanted to get to the house of the safe witch and back in daylight.

Tim went upstairs. He couldn't go out and leave Sebastian curled up on his bed!

Sebastian was fast asleep, but he heard Tim open the door.

He looked up, saw Tim, and began to purr.

"Come on, Sebastian," said Tim, picking him up and slipping him under his jacket. "Miss Miff doesn't like you any more than she likes me, and I've got to get you out of here without her seeing me."

Tim was just crossing the hall to the front door, when Miss Miff came out of her room.

"Tim!" she said, as soon as she saw him. "Tim, come here. I want to talk to you."

Miss Miff looked at him. Her eyes seemed to bore into him.

"*What* have you got under your coat?" she said.

Tim felt Sebastian twitch.

There was a loud crash from Miss Miff's room.

"Whatever's that?" cried Miss Miff. She turned, and rushed back into her room.

Tim didn't wait to find out what had happened. He slipped out of the front door.

Sebastian jumped out of his coat, and ran off to Mr. Berryman's house for breakfast.

Tim ran out of The Yard, and along the canal. The thunder storm had cleared the air. The sun was shining and even the streets of the town looked bright. Two dogs were playing on the pavement. Tim stopped to look at them. A boy rode past on a bicycle, whistling as he went.

Tim had felt tired to begin with, but now he felt better. He began to run.

Tim had slowed down to a walk long before he left the town. But at last the sheds and factories were behind him, and he was walking along the canal bank beside the back yards of houses. And then there were trees along the bank, and grass, and he was in the country. He could still see houses along the road to his right, but there was a field in between.

Tim saw a tree trunk lying across the path, and sat down on it to eat his sandwich. He looked at the tree trunk very carefully before he sat down. But it was just a tree trunk, and as he sat there in the sunlight he felt as if he had never heard of the stump people.

Tim didn't stop long. He kept his apple for the long walk home, and set off again down the path.

He came to the lock gates.

There was no one there. The sky was blue overhead. The sun shone down on the grass, and the water lapped against the gates.

Tim stood looking at them, and wondering for a moment if the Hidden People were all a kind of dream.

Then he saw the willow tree. He remembered how he and Captain Jory and Tobias had hidden under it. He remembered how frightened the people at the lock gates had been, when they saw Jack.

"It's no dream," he said aloud. "And I must get to Melinda's house and back in daylight, or I shall find that out again tonight."

He set off down the path at a run.

Tim saw Hollow Hill, away across the canal to his left. The path by the canal was still in sunshine, but Hollow Hill itself was in shadow.

Tim shivered.

As he looked at the ring of trees on top of the hill, he saw a sudden yellow glow. Smoke drifted up over the trees.

Someone had lit a fire on the top of Hollow Hill.

The day suddenly seemed colder.

Tim shivered again, and ran on along the path by the canal.

He hadn't gone far, when he came to a clump of trees.

He stopped. "That cottage is in those trees," he said to himself. He remembered the little man and the stump people.

He went slowly over towards the trees. There was a little path towards them, and he followed it into the trees.

He came to a big patch of grass. This was where the cottage had been.

But there was nothing there now, except a few blocks of grey stone. The cottage had vanished.

Tim went back to the canal. The sun was still shining, as he went on along the path.

He was beginning to wonder if he would find Melinda's cottage, or if that would have vanished, too, when he saw a bridge over the canal ahead of him.

It was the bridge where he had seen the wild witches.

Melinda's cottage stood along the road to his right, just as Tim remembered it. He broke into a run.

When he got to the gate, he stopped. Now that he was there, Tim wasn't sure that he wanted to see Melinda. He wished he was safely home again.

"Still, I might as well go, now I'm here," Tim said to himself. He opened the gate, and went up the path to the door.

Knocker's face looked out at him from the brass knocker, just as it had done that night months ago, when he was there with Tobias.

The face seemed to be looking at Tim, and the eyes were very unfriendly indeed.

Tim picked up a stone, and banged on the door.

The door of the cottage slowly opened, and there was Melinda.

She looked just as Tim remembered her. She had the same long skirt, and the same ragged shawl, but Tim thought she looked a little more friendly than she had done before.

He was glad she did.

She gave him a long, long look, and then stepped back.

"Come in," she said.

The tiger-skin rug lay on the floor, just as he had remembered it. In spite of the sunshine, there was a good log fire blazing away. The firelight shone in the mirror and the brass candlesticks, and danced in the glass bottles along the shelves.

"Sit down," said Melinda.

Tim went over to a chair by the fire. He was careful not to step on the rug.

As he sat down, he saw that Melinda was watching him. She smiled. Some of her teeth were missing, but it was a friendly smile, and Tim felt a little better.

"Don't be afraid of the tiger," said Melinda. "He won't hurt you."

Tim wasn't sure about that, so he said nothing.

Melinda came slowly forward to a chair on the other side of the fire, and sat down.

"So you're going to help your friends among the Hidden People to get back to Hollow Hill, are you, Tim?" she said.

Tim nodded. "How did you know?" he asked.

"There's not much that I don't know about the Hidden People," said Melinda. "You need to keep an eye on them, Tim – even the best of them."

Tim said nothing, but he felt that she was right.

"How much do you want to send them back to the Hill, Tim?" Melinda asked suddenly. "Aren't you afraid to be out at night, with the Wild Witches about?"

Tim looked up. "Yes," he said. "But I've got to get the Hidden People back to Hollow Hill. A friend of mine lives in The Yard. They'll drive him away from his house, if they've nowhere else to go."

Melinda nodded slowly. "So that's it," she said. She sat looking into the fire for some time.

Tim said nothing. He waited, watching Melinda.

At last she turned and looked at him. "Very well, Tim," she said slowly. "I'll help you. But you must be the one to do it, and you must do it alone."

She got up and went over to a corner cupboard, which was hanging on the wall. She opened it, took out a dark wooden box, and gave it to Tim.

It was a very strange box. There was a carved wooden figure of a tiger on the lid.

"Open it, and give me what's inside," said Melinda.

Tim opened the box. There was a ball of white string inside. He took it out, and handed it to Melinda.

Melinda had taken a glass bowl from the shelves.

She set the ball of string in the bowl, and put it down on a little table.

She took a bottle from the shelves, and poured something from it over the string.

At once the room was lit by a flash of blue fire.

The string itself seemed like a ball of silver flames.

Then the fire died away. The ball of string lay in the bowl as before, but now it glowed and shone with silver fire, as if it had been made from moonbeams.

"Give me the box," said Melinda. Tim handed it to her. She put the silver string inside, shut the lid, and gave it back to him.

Melinda moved the glass bowl back to the shelf. She laid a blue cloth over the little table, and set three silver coins on the cloth.

The coins looked very old, and one of them had a hole in the middle.

Melinda held her hand out over the coins, and muttered something.

The coins shone brightly.

"Pick up the coins, Tim," said Melinda. "They will help to keep you safe. If anyone attacks you, throw one of the coins in his face, and you will go free."

Tim looked at the coins, and then at Melinda.

Melinda nodded. "Take them," she said.

Tim picked them up and put them in his pocket.

"Now," said Melinda, "This is what you must do. On the next night when the moon is full, you must make your way to the little bridge over the canal. You must keep on this side of the canal. Don't come by the road, and whatever happens, don't cross over the water. Go on past the bridge, till you come to the wood where you saw the wild witches.

"When the moon is full, the wild witches will be at the Seven Stones, which are in the middle of the wood. The Highwayman and his friends from Hollow Hill will be there too. Go on, past the wood, and you will find a field. In the middle of the field, there is a pool. A big stone juts out over the pool, and a little thorn tree grows beside it.

"Tie one end of the silver string to the little tree, and then creep back to the canal, letting the string out as you go. Creep all around the wood, up to the road and round the far side, and back to the pool in the field.

"Go back along the far side of the pool till you come to the thorn tree.

"Then take the key from your pocket, and pull the other end of the silver string through the hole in the end of the key. The silver string will slip through wood and stone, but the wild witches and the Highwayman and his friends cannot cross it. It will drive them out of the wood and across the field and into the pool. And that will be the end of them.

"When they are all gone, put the string back into the box, and toss it after them into the pool."

"But – do you mean they'll all be drowned?" asked Tim.

Melinda looked at him. "Don't you want to kill them, Tim?" she asked.

Tim thought for a moment. "I want them to go away. But I don't think I want to kill them," he said. "I don't like killing things."

Melinda smiled, as if pleased. She nodded her head. "You can't kill them, Tim," she said. "You can only change them. You'll see. They won't drown – I promise you that. But they will change."

"How?" asked Tim.

"The whispering trees will tell you," said Melinda. "When you have heard the trees whispering, you can go home."

"I don't understand," said Tim.

"You will," said Melinda. "Take the box and go now. I want you to be home before dark. And go by the road, Tim, not the canal."

"There are some of the Highwayman's friends watching me in The Yard," said Tim. "And the moon won't be full for days yet."

"It is seven days till the moon is full," said Melinda. "You must hide, Tim. We must hide you for seven days."

"But where?" asked Tim.

Melinda thought for a moment. Then she nodded her head.

"I shall see you are hidden where your friends can find you, but where the wild witches can't come," she said. "Go home now, Tim, and remember: take the box with the silver string with you wherever you go. *Wherever* you go, mind! And don't be afraid. Tomorrow you will be in hiding."

"But where am I going?" asked Tim.

"Home," said Melinda. "Goodnight."

She opened the front door, and Tim went out.

To Tim's surprise, the sun was still shining. He tucked the box under his jacket, and set off for the main road. He looked back to wave, but Melinda had shut the door.

Tim held the box with one hand, and pulled his apple out with the other. He was hungry.

He hadn't gone far along the road, when Mr. Penny's lorry pulled up in front of him.

"Hallo, Tim," called Mr. Penny, leaning out of the window. "Want a ride into town?"

"Yes, please!" said Tim, running along to the cab, and climbing in.

He kept the wooden box under his jacket. The lorry jerked forward, and Mr. Penny set off for the town.

Tim found Sebastian curled up on his bed, when he took his supper upstairs that night. He couldn't think how Sebastian had got there, but he was very glad to see him.

As he took a last look out of the window, Tim saw Arun's torch circling in the window across The Yard. He swung his own torch in a circle.

There were two short flashes from Arun's window. Tim flashed back once. Then he switched the top of the torch to green, and swung it in a circle again. Arun flashed a green circle back at him.

Tim put the catch on the window, and set the wooden bar across the door. He put the three silver coins into the wooden box with the silver string, and slipped the box into the bed. Then he got into bed himself.

He ate his supper, and went to sleep with his arm round the box, and with Sebastian pressed up against his feet, purring.

RED RIDING HOOD

a play

The Cast

- Narrator
- Little Red
- Mother
- Grandma
- Wolf
- Woodcutter
- Chorus

Narrator: Once upon a time, there was a little girl known as Red Riding Hood. One day, her mother asked her to visit her grandma, who lived on the other side of the woods.

Mother: Grandma hasn't been feeling well. I told her you would take her some nice food for lunch.

Little Red: I'll go right away.
I love visiting Grandma!

Mother: Be sure to stay on the path.
Don't go into the woods.

Little Red: Don't worry, Mother.
I'll do as you say.

Narrator: But Red Riding Hood hadn't gone far when she saw some pretty flowers growing near the path.

Little Red: What lovely flowers! I'll pick some for Grandma.

Narrator: As Red Riding Hood happily picked more and more flowers, she forgot what her mother had said. Soon she had wandered deep into the woods.

Chorus: Watch out, watch out,
Red Riding Hood!
There's a wolf nearby –
and he's up to no good!

Narrator: Sure enough, a wolf was watching Red Riding Hood. He was lean and mean and *hungry*!

Wolf (to himself): Yum! A tasty little girl!

Narrator: Putting on his best smile, the wolf strolled over to Red Riding Hood.

Wolf: Hello, dear child. Where are you going?

Little Red: I'm going to visit my grandma. She's not feeling well.

Wolf: Where does your grandma live, my dear?

Little Red: She lives on the other side of the woods, in the cottage by the old mill.

Chorus: Oh no! Oh no!
Now *he* knows where to go!

Little Red: I must find my way back to the path now, or I'll be late.

Wolf: Let me help. I can show you a *short* way to your grandma's.

Narrator: Of course, the cunning wolf
sent Red Riding Hood
the *longest* way.
Then *he* took the short way
to Grandma's house.
He knocked on the door.

Grandma: Is that you,
Little Red Riding Hood?

Wolf (in a little voice): Yes, Grandma.

Grandma: Lift up the latch, my dear,
and come in.

Narrator: In went the wolf!

Grandma (horrified): Aaagh!

Narrator: Grandma jumped out of bed and hid in the first place she could find.

Wolf: I'll get *you* later, Grandma.

Narrator: At that very moment, Red Riding Hood knocked on the door. The wolf quickly climbed into bed and pulled the blankets up to his whiskery chin.

Wolf (pretending to be Grandma): Who is it?

Chorus: Watch out, watch out,
Red Riding Hood!
The wolf's in the house,
and he's up to no good!

Little Red: It's Red Riding Hood, Grandma.

Wolf: Lift up the latch, my dear, and come in.

Narrator: Red Riding Hood went in and sat on the bed.

Little Red: Grandma! Mother told me you were not well – and you *do* look different!

Wolf: Don't worry. I'll be better soon. Come closer, my dear.

Little Red: But Grandma, what big ears you have!

Wolf: All the better to *hear* you with, my dear.

Little Red: But Grandma, what big eyes you have!

Wolf: All the better to *see* you with, my dear.

Little Red: Oh, but Grandma, what big *teeth* you have!

Wolf: All the better to EAT you with, my dear!

Little Red: Oh no!

Narrator: The wolf jumped out of bed and grabbed Red Riding Hood.

Little Red: Aaaagh! AAAAGH!

Narrator: Just then, a woodcutter was passing the cottage. He heard the screams and rushed inside...and saw the wolf.

Little Red: Help! Help!

Woodcutter (angrily): What are you up to, Wolf?

Narrator: The wolf took one look at the furious woodcutter and ran for his life.

Woodcutter (to wolf): I'll get you later!

(to Little Red): Are you all right?

Little Red: Yes, I'm all right now, but he was going to *eat* me!

Grandma (stepping from her hiding place): Me, too!

Little Red: Grandma! Thank goodness you're safe. I thought he might have eaten you already.

Woodcutter: You are both *very* lucky that I was passing by.

Narrator: To celebrate, they all shared the food that Red Riding Hood had brought. Then the woodcutter took Red Riding Hood home – and set off to fix that big bad wolf for good.